Two Little Witchlings
BOOK OF SHADOWS

A Grimoire of
beginners spells, magic basics
& Pagan traditions!

Welcome, Little Witchlings!

Paganism is an umbrella term that covers most beliefs relating to the natural world & the Old Ways. However, each Pagan individual might use another "label" in order to identify themselves. Some of these labels are Wiccan, Druid, Heathen, Shaman, Wyrdist & Witch!

Pagans that also identify as having magickal abilities tend to practice Witchcraft. Witches sometimes have a Book of Shadows, or a "Grimoire" to keep their knowledge in.

This is yours. Enjoy ✨

Contents

1) What is Magick?

2) Who Can Be a Witch?

3) Witches Calendar; Sabbats

4) Moon Phases & Their Magickal Meanings

5) Astrological Signs; The Zodiacs

6) Chakra Magick - What Are Chakra's Anyway?

7) Calling the Corners

8) Casting a Circle

9) Creating Your Own Altar Space!

10) Candle Colours (Don't Play With Matches)

11) Water Magick (Collect Responsibly)

12) Crystals; Starting a Collection

13) Herbs & Spices; Your Own Apothecary!

14) Natural Remedies For Common Ailments

15) Basic Spells That Are Ready To Go

16) Creating Your Own Spells!

17) Hexes, Curses & Karma; Handle With Care

18) Write Your Own Hexes!

19) Sigil Magick; A Basic Understanding

20) Create Your Own Sigils!

21) Divination ('mancy galore!)

22) Auras; How To Read Them & What They Mean

23) Spirit Guides - Who's Your Animal Totem?

24) Witchionary - The A-Z of Magickal Words!

1) What is Magick?

Hocus Pocus, Charmed, Sabrina the Teenage Witch.. all strong & powerful witches who could perform the greatest of tricks from creating things out of thin air to moving objects across the room to shapeshifting.

But real life magick is nowhere near as theatrical (if only!). That doesn't make it any less *real.*

There are some people that are born with magickal abilities. They can predict the future through divination, talk to the dead through mediumship, feel exactly what another person is feeling as an Empath, and even channel light itself through Reiki, as well as lots & lots of other very real ways of using magick every day.

Everyone else is born with the ability to step into their own power, develop their craft, and master their gifts in time. But not every person wants to do this. Some just don't believe it's possible at all, and that magick is just make-believe. Others think it's bad or "evil" in some way (it's not) and are afraid that something bad will happen to them. And there are others who know that it's real, but, don't wish to pursue a life full of magick for many different reasons.

This Book of Shadows is here to accompany you on your own magickal journey as you discover your mystical talents & learn to nurture them. Let's get started!

2) Who Can Be a Witch?

You probably have this idea that only haggard green women with warts & grey hair can be Witches, right?

That is a very negative, fake view that is historically put in people's minds so that Witches are seen as evil tricksters that are to be feared & avoided at all costs. Not true at all.

The truth is there are Witches everywhere. They are regular people that you see every day! Girls, boys, women, men, librarians, chemists, doctors, cashiers, farmers, builders, teachers, tech support.. we are in every corner of society, living regular lives. The only real difference between us and "normies" (non-magickal folk) is we have not only accepted our power, but stepped into it. We love Nature and all her gifts, we do good things and hope every day to help make the world a better, kinder, nicer, tidier, more tolerant place to live. After all, this is the only home we have.

Anybody can be a Witch. Your gender, your skin colour and your identity have absolutely no impact on the world of Magick. As long as you respect nature, treat all animals with kindness, don't drop litter, don't be wasteful, share the resources... there's no reason at all why you can't be a part of this community.

Which Witch Are They?

Think about some of the people in your life who give off a bit of a magickal vibe. Could they be a Witch? Use this space to write down who you'd have in your ideal Coven, and why! ✦

3) Witches Calendar: Wheel of the Year

The Wheel of the Year is made of Sabbats (festivals) that mark the changing seasons. Starting in December, eight festivals spaced roughly 6-8 weeks apart are celebrated every year by Pagans all over the world. Two mark the Equinoxes, two mark the Solstices, two mark the thinning of the veils, & two mark masculine/feminine deities that represent the changing of the seasons. See below for more information on each Sabbat, when it occurs, & what we do!

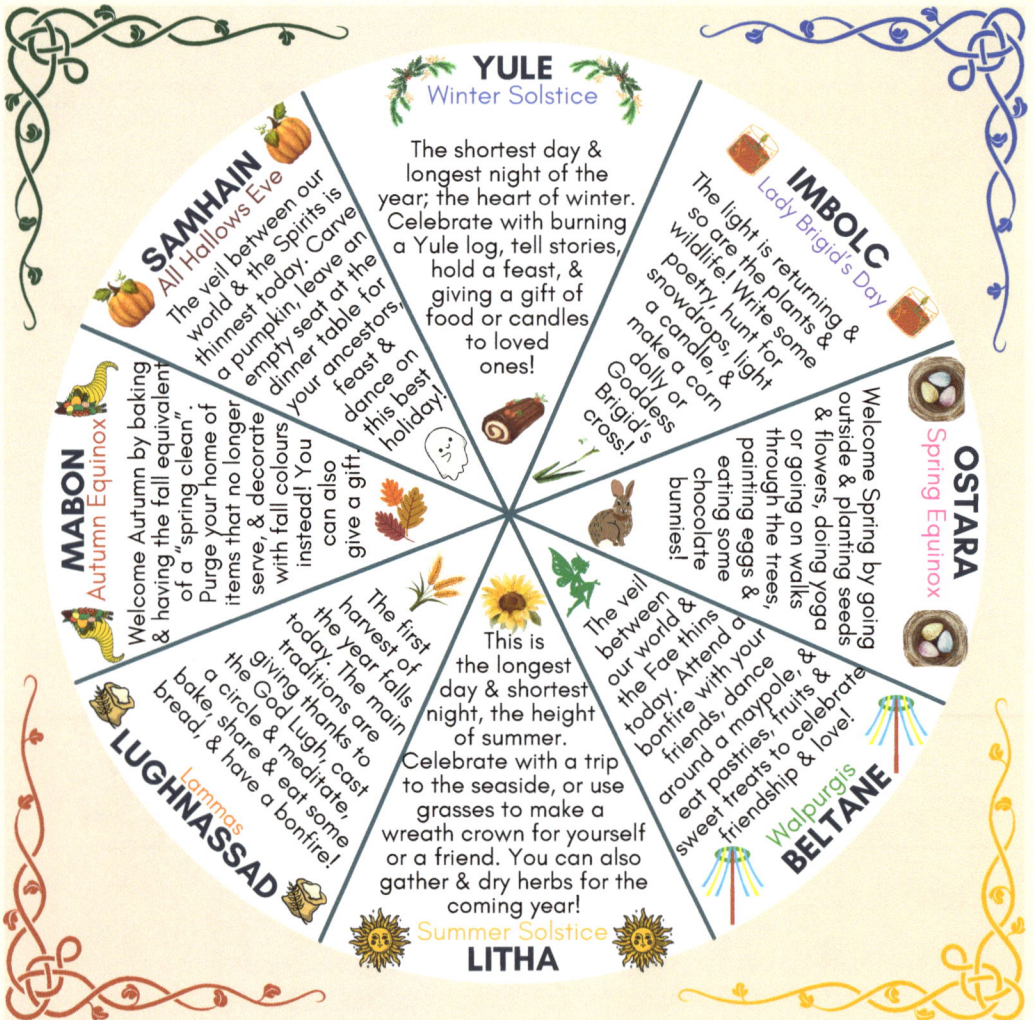

YULE
Winter Solstice

The shortest day & longest night of the year; the heart of winter. Celebrate with burning a Yule log, tell stories, hold a feast, & giving a gift of food or candles to loved ones!

SAMHAIN
All Hallows Eve

The veil between our world & the Spirits is thinnest today. Carve a pumpkin, leave an empty seat at the dinner table for your ancestors, feast & dance on this best holiday! You can also give a gift instead!

MABON
Autumn Equinox

Welcome Autumn by baking & having the fall equivalent of a "spring clean". Purge your home of items that no longer serve, & decorate with fall colours instead!

LUGHNASSAD
Lammas

The first harvest of the year falls today. The main traditions are giving thanks to the God Lugh, cast a circle & meditate, bake, share & eat some bread, & have a bonfire!

LITHA
Summer Solstice

This is the longest day & shortest night, the height of summer. Celebrate with a trip to the seaside, or use grasses to make a wreath crown for yourself or a friend. You can also gather & dry herbs for the coming year!

BELTANE
Walpurgis

The veil between our world & the Fae thins today. Attend a bonfire with your friends, dance around a maypole, & eat pastries, fruits, & sweet treats to celebrate friendship & love!

OSTARA
Spring Equinox

Welcome Spring by going outside & planting seeds & flowers, doing yoga or going on walks through the trees, painting eggs & eating some chocolate bunnies!

IMBOLC
Lady Brigid's Day

The light is returning & so are the plants & wildlife. Write some poetry, light a candle, hunt for snowdrops, & make a corn dolly or Goddess Brigid's cross!

Witchling's Calendar: Your Celebration Ideas!

This is your space to come up with ways to celebrate each Sabbat in your own way. Perhaps you wish to acknowledge them as a solitary Pagan, or perhaps you could do it with family & friends? Would you like to travel somewhere special like Stonehenge or would you prefer to stay home and have a big feast? Perhaps you could do something for charity? See what you come up with!

YULE

LITHA

IMBOLC

LAMMAS

OSTARA

MABON

BELTANE

SAMHAIN

Witchling's Calendar: Thinning Of The Veils

Twice a year, it is said that the veils between world's grow really thin. This is because the ancient Celts only had 2 seasons instead of 4. At the threshold of Winter (Samhain), huge feasts celebrated the ancestors, & care was taken to avoid the restless dead. At the threshold of Summer (Beltane), massive celebrations were held to honour the magic of Nature as well as it's protectors. Use this space to record your sightings, experiences & interactions with the **Spirits** of October & the **Fae** of May.

HALLOWEEN / SAMHAIN

BELTANE / MAY-EVE

Arty Activity

Bring this page & poem to life with colour...

Into the forest I eagerly stroll
To lose my mind & find my soul
Replace the sounds of greed & unease
With flowing of water & rustle of trees

I leave behind a world of turmoil
Step off the cement & onto the soil
Take time out of the world's rat race
watch the squirrels as they play & chase

Feel the magick of nature's world
watch the clouds billow & twirl
Take this moment to top up your soul
walk through the kingdom of Spirits of Old

4) Moon Phases

The Moon is not just a rock that circulates our world. She is vital part of not just life on Earth, but every practicing Witch & Witchling. Lunar Magick is something that is both joyful & fulfilling, & certain spells are naturally stronger if performed under specific phases of the moon. But what does each moon phase mean? What even *are* the moon's phases?

Let's start with the terms. You have "new", "full", "waxing", "waning", "crescent" & "gibbous". Okay, cool. So let's define those:
NEW - When the moon sits between us & the sun, & can't be seen.
FULL - The moon is now on the other side, & can be seen in full!
WAXING - This refers to a growing of the moon's image (right side).
WANING - This refers to a shrinking of the moon's image (left side).
CRESCENT - Means less than half of the moon is lit up by the sun.
GIBBOUS - Means more than half of the moon is lit up by the sun.

Now we have the terms defined, what exactly is the order? Here is a visual diagram to help you. It starts with the New Moon!

New Moon

Waxing Crescent

Waning Crescent

First Quarter

Last Quarter

Waxing Gibbous

Waning Gibbous

Full Moon

Now let's discuss what each Moon Phase means, how it impacts us and our magick, and why it makes some spells stronger!

NEW MOON - The New Moon signifies the seeds of intention for new beginnings. It's a great time to start new projects, & set new goals.

WAXING CRESCENT - Time you ask yourself what you're doing to complete your goals. Are you taking the steps necessary? The waxing Moon will inspire you to see them through, & you must do so.

FIRST QUARTER - This D-shaped Moon is calling you to to visualize what's happening energetically — you're building momentum toward your intentions as the moon gets bigger. Keep up the good work!

WAXING GIBBOUS - During this phase, you start making moves — prioritize, make plans, start taking practical steps toward your intentions. This is the final step before manifestation.

FULL MOON - This Moon represents fulfilment, the completion of your desires, & the peak of progress. Time to evaluate & reflect.

WANING GIBBOUS - This time is for releasing anything that is not serving your spiritual journey. Be ruthless with it. Drop any bad vibes!

LAST QUARTER - This Moon calls us to start looking inwards, check in with the results of previous spells. and start preparing for the new beginnings that are to come.

WANING CRESCENT - This phase is geared toward evaluating old habits and patterns that have run their course, letting them go, & starting to explore your intentions for the next New Moon!

5) Astrological Signs
- The Zodiacs

Aquarius	Pisces	Aries	Taurus
Gemini	Cancer	Leo	Virgo
Libra	Scorpio	Sagittarius	Capricorn

Aquarius – 21 January - 19 February (The *Water-bearer*)

Pisces – 20 February - 20 March (The *Fish*)

Aries – 21 March - 20 April (The *Ram*)

Taurus – 21 April - 21 May (The *Bull*)

Gemini – 22 May - 21 June (The *Twins*)

Cancer – 22 June - 23 July (The *Crab*)

Leo – 24 July - 23 August (The *Lion*)

Virgo – 24 August - 23 September (The *Maiden*)

Libra – 24 September - 22 October (The *Scales*)

Scorpio – 23 October - 22 November (The *Scorpion*)

Sagittarius – 23 November - 21 December (The *Archer*)

Capricorn – 22 December - 20 January (The *Goat*)

In astronomy & astrology, the zodiac is like a belt of space that circles around the Earth & signifies the Sun's annual path. 12 groups of stars lie in the zodiac. Each of these constellations occupies a 12th of the circle, & has been given a name & a set of dates that mark the time when the Sun passes through that constellation. Those born under each zodiac have particular traits & sets of skills, that tend to make up a portion of their personality.

Using the information on the previous page, this space is for you to write down the Zodiac signs of the people in your life! You can work out people's zodiacs by finding out their birthday, and then seeing which dates their birthday fall between on the astrology calendar.

My Zodiac is:

_____ Zodiac is:

_____ Zodiac is:

_____ Zodiac is:

_____ Zodiac is:

_____ Zodiac is:

_____ Zodiac is:

_____ Zodiac is:

6) Chakra Magick - What Are Chakras?

The word "Chakra" is translated as meaning "spinning wheel of energy". They are energy centers located along the spine. Just like a wheel, our energy can flow, go too fast, or get stuck! A wheel is a solid object that needs energy to function. We are no different. Let's explore the Chakra (pronounced 'shack-ra') system together!

Crown Chakra — Connection, Imagination, Dreams

Third Eye Chakra — Intuition, Wisdom, Mindfulness

Throat Chakra — Expression, Communication, Truth

Heart Chakra — Love, Empathy, Compassion

Solar Plexus Chakra — Instinct, Confidence, Resilience

Sacral Chakra — Joy, Fun, Play, Creativity, Identity

Root Chakra — Power, Security, Roots, Strength

The **Crown** is located at the top of the head. You can connect with it by daydreaming, & clear it with meditation & Dream Journaling.
The **Third Eye** is located between the eyebrows. You can connect with it with breathing exercises, & clear it by eating purple foods!
The **Throat** is located in your neck. You can connect with it by singing, & clear it by saying affirmations out loud for 3 minutes.
The **Heart** is located in your chest. You can connect with it by doing some Yoga, & clear it by writing in a Gratitude Journal.
The **Solar Plexus** is located in the tummy. You can connect with it by using citrus essential oil, & clear it by wearing yellow clothes!
The **Sacral** is located in the pelvis. You can connect with it by swimming/having a bath, & clear it by eating a sweet treat.
The **Root** is located at the base of the spine. Connect with it by gardening/planting, & clear it by Grounding yourself!

My Chakra Journal

This page is for your own Chakra Cleansing & Connection. Use the boxes provided to create your own Energy information!

	Foods that I can eat	Colours that I can wear	Activities that I can do
Crown Chakra			
Third Eye Chakra			
Throat Chakra			
Heart Chakra			
Solar Plexus Chakra			
Sacral Chakra			
Root Chakra			

7) Calling the Corners

There are 4 basic elements in the natural world that tie in with Magic; these are Earth, Air, Fire & Water.

EARTH: Spirit of the North, Earth reflects strength & grounding. Zodiac signs that fall under this element are Taurus, Virgo, & Capricorn.

AIR: Spirit of the East, Air reflects Inspiration & cleansing. Zodiac signs that fall under this element are Gemini, Libra, Aquarius.

FIRE: Spirit of South, Fire reflects passion & energy. Zodiac signs that fall under this element are Aries, Leo, & Sagittarius.

WATER: Spirit of the West, Water reflects creation & power. Zodiac signs that fall under this element are Cancer, Scorpio, & Pisces.

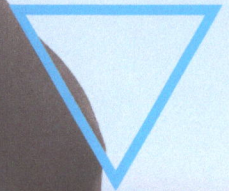

The simplest way to Call the Corners is to have a representation of each Element facing the correct direction in your home. For example; a rock facing North, a feather facing East, a candle facing South, & a jar of water facing West!

8) Casting a Circle

Some witches & other neo-pagans cast sacred circles before using magick or performing rituals. The circle acts as a portal to the realms of the deities & spirits, as a protection against negative energy & bad intentions, & as a mental tool to put you in the right state of mind. Casting a circle can be as simple or complex as you like, using lots of objects or none at all.

OPENING YOUR CIRCLE

First, find a safe, private place to cast your circle. Next, purify the place where you will cast your circle by tidying the area up, then sprinkling some salt and/or essential oil.

After this you need to create the physical boundary of your circle. If you're inside, this can be with crystals or just some string (make sure you tie it!), if you're outside you can use things from nature such as rocks or twigs.

Once that's done, collect your objects you intend to use (such as candles, salt, crystals, herbs/spices, feathers, pinecones & witches bells) and create your Altar at the centre of the circle. Once you begin your Ritual, don't leave the circle until it's completed. Place an object that represents a Corner in the correct direction (Earth = North, Air = East, Fire = South, Water = West). Light your candles if you are using any, clear your mind, and state your intentions clearly & confidently. You have now cast your circle and are ready to perform your ritual!

CLOSING YOUR CIRCLE

You have invoked the Elements, called to your chosen Deities, and finished your spell. Now what?

It is very important to close your circle before stepping out of it. Pay your respects, give thanks, and then close by saying "So Mote It Be" & blow out your candle(s). Remember to double check your candles have gone out fully, & run used matches under the tap.

9) Creating your own Altar space

Setting up your very own, very first Altar space is really important. It should be a sacred space in which you feel supported, safe, happy and free to be yourself!

Having a home altar is a way to connect to your spirituality on a daily basis. It can be used to practice magic, meditate, & connect with the divine or your ancestors.

Altars do not need to be huge, expensive, or elaborate. You can literally create an Altar in drawer, a jar, on a shelf, or in a shoebox that can be kept under your bed. There's no right or wrong way to create your sacred space.

Basics:
★ **Have a focal point**. This can be a statue, an ornament, a decorative candle, a pretty rock or favourite crystal!
★ **Choose an Altar cloth** to cover the space. Make sure it's safe for lit candles, wax drippings, & incense, should you use any.
★ **Call the Corners** to increase your connection to the elements. Figure out where North is, and from there, have something on each direction to represent Earth, Air, Fire & Water.

badabing, badaboom, you have an Altar! Decorate it as much as you like with whatever you like. It's important that you're happy with it. You can change it up every season, add specific items to honour each Sabbat, and allow it to grow and change along with you.

Design Your Altar space

Use this page to design, draw & colour your perfect Altar space. It can be as simple or as fancy as you envision!

10) Candle Colours

Every colour has a different meaning and can enhance your spell work if used correctly. Remember; there's no such thing as doing a spell wrong, it's all about the intent. A white candle can be used to replace any other colour, and carving symbols or runes into the candle before use will only strengthen it. **Use matches with care!!**

RED:
Courage
Passion
Charisma
Energy
Strength
Fast Action

ORANGE:
Success
Prosperity
Ambition
Justice
Positivity
Opportunity

YELLOW:
Clarity
Knowledge
Focus
Memory
Reasoning
Manifesting

GREEN:
Growth
Luck
Fertility
Abundance
Healing
Grounding

BLUE:
Spirituality
Creativity
Harmony
Inspiration
Unblock
Flow

PURPLE:
Development
Psychic
Awareness
Authority
Wisdom
Influence

PINK:
Romance
Friendship
Balance
Nurturing
Healing
Happiness

WHITE:
Meditation
Protection
Healing
Cleansing
Peace
Purity

BLACK:
Banishing
Hexing
Warding
Protection
Binding
Blocking

BROWN:
Concentration
Security
Animals
Stability
Grounding
Connection

SILVER:
Resolve Conflict
Dream Work
Moon Spells
Psychic Boost
Femininity
Intuition

GOLD:
Fame/Fortune
Power
Sun Spells
Success
Masculinity
Prosperity

Arty Activity

This is your space to create freely!

11) Water Magick

Water is a precious gift from the earth. It can put out fire, carve it's way through stone, even destroy iron, & when trapped, water makes a new path. It represents going with the flow, shaping your own destiny, & stepping into your own power. Magickal water is a great resource for spell work. **Collect water responsibly!!**

MOON WATER:
Charging
Blessing
Cleansing
Powering
Healing
Femininity

SUN WATER:
Happiness
Creativity
Fertility
Sparking
Courage
Clairvoyance

RAIN WATER:
Growth
Rebirth
Scrying
Ritual Work
Cleansing
Altar Work

STORM WATER:
Vitality
Self-esteem
Courage
Protection
Strength
Speedy results

DEW WATER:
Fae Work
Fertility
Growth
New Moon
Healing
New Beginnings

SNOW WATER:
Transformation
Peace
Unthawing
Cooling Spell
Balance
Ending Spells

OCEAN WATER:
Manifestation
Protecting
Banishing
Cleansing
Healing
Emotional Health

RIVER WATER:
Meditation
Charging
Breakthrough
Encourage
Power
Moving On

LAKE WATER:
Reflection
Recovery
Relaxation
Protection
Contentment
Bring Peace

WELL WATER:
Concentration
Wishes
Dream Work
Depth
Grounding
Connection

SPRING WATER:
Abundance
Growth
Cleansing
Potions
Femininity
Waxing Moon Work

SWAMP WATER:
Cursing
Binding
Banishing
Hexing
Masculinity
Waning Moon Work

Witchling Water

Use this space to write down where/when you collected your magickal waters from, how you charged it (if it's sun or moon water) & what you plan to use it for! **Always ask your grown-up first.**

12) Crystals

Crystals are solidified minerals from deep within the earth. They hold magickal properties that emit their own energy, and this energy can be used for a wide variety of things. They have been used for millennia as talismans, in jewelry, and as charms. The most popular is Clear Quartz, which can be used to replace any other gemstone.

QUARTZ:
Amplifying other crystals, clearing energy, manifesting intentions, clear the mind.

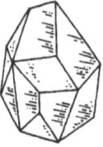

CITRINE:
Abundance & prosperity, wealth, success, clarity & imagination boost.

TIGERS EYE:
Increased focus, self confidence, perseverance, balance, grounding, gut instinct.

CARNELIAN:
Concentration, creativity & divination, ancestor work, courage & confidence.

JASPER:
Warrior strength & motivation, spiritual awakening & visioning, earth energy.

AVENTURINE:
Compassion, leadership & perseverance, vitality, optimism & confidence in yourself.

MALACHITE:
Transformation, change & growth, acceptance, go with the flow, trust your Path.

LAPIS LAZULI:
Vision & psychic awareness, higher self, divination, promotes connection.

TOURMALINE:
Stabilization, calming, clarity & clearing tension, truth, honest communication.

KYANITE:
Wards off energy vampires, shields you, filters negativity, enhances dream work.

OBSIDIAN:
Blocks negativity & returns to sender, purify, protection & grounding, power enhance.

ROSE QUARTZ:
Peace & calm, emotional healing, unconditional love, friendship, trust & strength.

Your Crystals

The crystals named on the previous page are the most common, most popular, or easiest to get your hands on from any Witchy type shop. But there's bound to be others in your collection, or others you have your eye on! Use this section to create your own information chart. Don't forget to give them colour, & add what they mean!

_____:

_____:

_____:

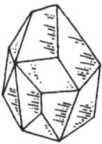

_____:

_____:

_____:

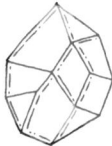

_____:

_____:

_____:

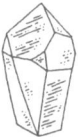

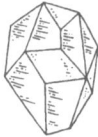

_____:

_____:

_____:

13) Herbs & Spices

Herbs have been used in witchcraft since the Old Ways. They can be grown or foraged, traded or purchased, fresh or dried. They can be used in every spell you could possibly think of, and bring a little something different to each one. The most important thing is your intention, so don't worry too much. **If you're unsure, check!!**

PROTECTION:
Lavendar
Rosemary
Basil
Salt
Sage
Mint

SUCCESS:
Bay Leaf
Chamomile
St Johns Wort
Buttercups
Rosemary
Fennel Leaf

GROWTH:
Spearmint
Cinnamon
Coriander
Chives
Parsley
Thyme

CHANGE:
Oregano
Coriander
Tarragon
Rosemary
Dandelion
Garlic

LUCK:
Ginger
Basil
Parsley
Turmeric
Mugwort
Strawberry leaf

WISDOM:
Dill
Parsley
All Spice
Nutmeg
Thyme
Cumin

LOVE:
Coriander
Cinnamon
Vanilla
Caraway
Mustard
Rose Petal

PEACE:
Fennel leaf
Clary Sage
Lemon Balm
Apple seeds
Chamomile
Salt

HEALTH:
Cinnamon
Sage
Ginger
Garlic
Salt
Honey

HEALING:
Lavender
Coriander
Flax seed
Chamomile
Honey
All Spice

DIVINATION:
Rhubarb
Sea Salt
Eggshell
Yarrow
Rosehips
Dandelion

COURAGE:
Bay Leaf
Paprika
Peppercorns
Rosemary
Mint
Nettle

Your Apothecary

It's such an exciting feeling when you first begin your Apothecary. There are just a *feeeew* **very important** rules that go with the responsibility of having one though...

Only take what you need. If you are foraging, never take too much from Nature, because not only is it wasteful, it deprives others from using it, including wild animals that may rely on it.

Never eat anything unless you are 100% sure it is safe. This one is probably THE most important. Before you put anything in your mouth, know what it is, and definitely check with your grown up. There are all sorts of toxins & poisons out there, so be safe!

Store herbs & spices responsibly. If you want to keep your foodstuffs fresh, simply put them in a glass jar of clean water and secure the lid properly, or loosely wrap them in a damp paper towel and keep them in a tightly sealed container or reusable bag in the fridge (ask your grown up if taking up fridge space is okay). If you wish to dry them out, you can either lay them in a single layer on a baking sheet & oven-dry them, or tie them in bunches above a window where the sun shines through (this is the cheapest, healthiest way, but will take a bit longer).

Check your herbs & spices regularly for unwanted guests. If your herb bunch is diseased or contains rot, it needs to be immediately binned & the bag/box it was stored in washed thoroughly. If you accidently brought home a critter or two, shake the plant carefully out of an open window until they fall off, or if you're uncomfortable doing that, ask your grown up to take the little creature outside. Remember to treat all souls kindly, no matter how big or small!

Use this space to write down where/when you foraged your herbs, how/where you've stored them, & what you plan to use it for!
Always ask your grown-up first. Check you know what's what!

Use this space to write down where/when you foraged your herbs,
how/where you've stored them, & what you plan to use it for!
Always ask your grown-up first. Check you know what's what!

14) Natural Remedies

Even the most powerful of Witches & cleanest of Pagans get sick from time to time. That's why it's super important to tell your grown-up right away so that they can determine if you need to see a doctor. There are some illnesses, however, that can be managed perfectly fine by Mother Nature herself. Let's take a look.

Hayfever

Eating a spoonful of genuine honey from the season every day will raise your pollen tolerance levels.

Colds/Flu

Lots of garlic & ginger, fresh lemon, raw honey, hot baths, and lots & lots of naps!

Sore Throat

Gargling with warm salt water with a little squeeze of fresh lemon juice helps a lot.

Nausea

Feeling sick is rotten. Tiny bites of either crystalized ginger or ginger biscuits will soothe nausea.

Headache

Smelling fresh lavender or boiling it with some coconut oil then rubbing it (cooled!) on your pulse points helps.

Sore Joints

Make a balm with rosemary & coconut oil (ask your adult to help) & rub it on your achy joints.

Diarrhea

Eating some good probiotic natural yogurt with syrup of elderflower will set your gut right again!

Insomnia

Struggling to sleep? Try some chamomile tea just before bedtime. It will soothe you nicely.

Eczema

Tea-tree oil will help with itchy skin. It's also great for helping cuts & grazes heal a little bit quicker.

Eating lots of fresh fruits & veggies every day, getting a good amount of sleep, & keeping yourself active, gives your body the best chances against most illnesses! But, you already knew that.

Witchling's Remedies

Use this space to write down any natural remedies & recipes that you hear from an elder or learn about by yourself. Remember to check with your grown up before using medicinal creations!

_____

Arty Activity

Bring this page to life with colour...

15) Basic Spells

Spellwork does **not** need to be elaborate, complicated or expensive. You can perform the simplest of Magick during the most mundane of activities;

- Stirring your day's desires into your morning cuppa!
- Dressing in colours that match your intentions!
- Drawing a sigil with your face cream or foundation before rubbing it in!
- Carrying a crystal that reflects what kind of energy you need for the day!
- Lighting a stick of incense & (very carefully) walking all around your space while saying positive messages out-loud such as: "I am open to any messages from the universe today".."I am powerful, I am strong, I am loved".."Negativity shall not harm my energy today"..

Is it nice to have all the gadgets & gizmo's galore? Sure it is. Is it fun to buy all of the things in order to make your spells look & feel more authentic? Absolutely. But the fact of the matter is, none of those things are necessary in order to perform Magick. The only thing that matters, literally the ONLY thing, is your **Intention**.

Intentions; Getting the wording right

With *any* kind of magick comes a good amount of responsibility. No spell should be cast at the expense of another person, unless it is a Hex or Curse (more on those kinds of spells later). Magick and Karma are deeply entwined (though there are those that would disagree strongly with this) and, if misused or cast through greed, selfishness, or any kind of viciousness that is unwarranted, the spell will not only fail, but it will teach you a valuable (& most likely harsh) lesson.

So, now that you know to use Magick with care, how about taking a look at some simple spells you can perform right now?

A Spell for Anger

Moon required; Full

Ingredients/Materials required; Paper, pen, heatproof bowl or container, matches, dried Sage.

Spell; *"I choose to release all anger and rage,*
My spirit is cleansed by fire & Sage!"

Instructions; First, write down the thing(s) that really ticked you off. Then tear up the paper and put it in a heatproof dish. Sprinkle the dried sage over the paper & ignite it. As the smoke curls towards the sky, say the Spell. Once only ashes are left, allow them to cool, & bury them in the earth or throw them in the bin.

A Spell for Anxiety

Moon required; New

Ingredients/Materials required; Sage, Rosemary or Lavender

Spell; *"By the root, by the flower,*
By the Goddess' healing power,
Calm & courage return to me,
Remove now my anxiety,
As I will it, so mote it be!"

Instructions; Hold the chosen herb in your left hand and hold it against your Solar Plexus Chakra (the Solar Plexus is located in your tummy just above your belly button). Concentrate on their smell, their feel, their energy. Envision their power seeping into you. Say the spell out loud. Envision that power now filling you from head to toe, leaving you in a golden light. The spell is now complete.

A Spell for Blessing a Space

Moon required; Any

Ingredients/Materials required; Incense, Matches

Spell; *"I cleanse any negative energy, as I will it, so mote it be."*

Instructions; Walk in a clockwise direction around the space you wish to cleanse, and say the spell out-loud while the smoke from the incense works it's way through the space. Handle fire with care!

A Spell for Banishing Negativity

Moon required; First Quarter or Last Quarter

Ingredients/Materials required; Salt, a broom

Spell; *"Swinging, sweeping, all around,*
Negativity banished, negativity bound,
Your power will vanish, you power will wane,
Only the good & the pure will remain."

Instructions; Sprinkle the salt across the doorway, then sweep the floor from East to West to whilst saying the spell.

A Spell to Create Change

Moon required; Full

Ingredients/Materials required; a cloth bag, a yellow ribbon.

Spell; *"The winds of Change around me blow,*
This rut I'm stuck in, with you now go,
I'll welcome your storm, I'll dance in your rain
I thank you right now for what I'm to gain!"

Instructions; Stand facing the wind and "capture" it in the bag. Say the spell. Close the bag & tie it with the ribbon. When you come across a situation that needs adapting, open the bag and "pour" forth the Winds of Change!

A Spell for Calling Your Power Back

Moon required; Waxing

Spell; *"I call my Power back to me,*
From all corners, sky, land & sea,
People, places, situations,
Realms & worlds in all directions,
I take control of what was drained,
Using knowledge I have gained,
Emotional Vampires siphon no more,
I block your feed forevermore,
I call my Power back to me,
As I will it, so mote it be!"

Instructions; Read the Spell aloud while facing the front door.

A Spell for Driving Fear Away

Moon required; Waning

Ingredients/Materials required; Nettle, Yarrow, small muslin bag.

Spell; *"Powers of light, magic of right, cast this Fright into forever's night!!"* – to be said 3 times.

Instructions; Place the herbs into the bag and hold it between your hands. Say the Spell. Keep the bag with you at all times, in your pocket or purse or backpack, or on a string/chain around your neck.

A Spell for De-stressing

Moon required; New

Ingredients/Materials required; Chamomile/ ginger/ honey tea.

Spell; *"Soothe my stress & cares away, urge me on to face the fray!"*

Instructions; Brew the tea, hold the mug to your nose with both hands & inhale the calming scents deeply while saying the spell.

A Spell for Finding Your Way

Moon required; Any

Ingredients/Materials required; None

Spell; *"With the power of my own might, may my heart & soul burn bright, May my instincts now come forth, bring me to my one true North!"*

Instructions; Read the Spell aloud while facing the North.

A Spell for Friendship

Moon required; Full

Ingredients/Materials required; Rose petals, apple slices, sage leaves, rosemary twigs, lavender.

Spell; *"A circle of friends is the circle of life, May these herbal gifts prevent any strife, we thank the Goddess for shining her light, bless our friendship to forever burn bright!"*

Instructions; Gather your friends, & create an image of a flower on the ground together out of the ingredients. Hold hands & walk or skip around the flower in a circle, saying the spell aloud.

A Spell for Luck

Moon required; Waxing

Ingredients/Materials required; 7 seeds (e.g. Nasturtium)

Spell; *"Luck be quick, Luck be kind, Luck be large, Luck be mine!"*

Instructions; Place the seeds on a clean windowsill, and let them sit under a full moon for at least 7 hours. Once they are fully charged, hold them in your hand, face a North-East direction (this direction is ideal for those seeking luck & fortune due to it's exposure to the morning sun) and say the spell out loud 3 times. Plant the seeds in the earth, and be on the look out for the blessings coming your way!

A Spell for Promoting Plant Growth

Moon required; Full

Ingredients/Materials required; A green candle, a clear quartz crystal, a seashell, & a jar of freshly charged Sun Water.

Spell; *"See this seed which I now sow,*
please allow this plant to grow,
grow it tall & fit & strong,
aid it's quest to live life long,
keep it grounded, help it thrive, Mother earth, help it survive!"

Instructions; Set your struggling plant on a west-facing windowsill, place the crystal on one side & the shell on the other. Light the candle, pour some Sun Water at the plants roots, and say the spell aloud. Blow out the candle. Don't move the crystal/shell for 5 days.

A Spell for Protection

Moon required; Any

Ingredients/Materials required; A crystal for protection (such as Obsidian, clear quartz or kyanite), salt, fresh mint & basil bunches.

Spell; *"I cast this circle round this place, no ills can enter my space,*
with herbs so rich & salt so pure, from all evils I'm secure!"

Instructions; Create a circle around you from the salt & herbs. Clear your mind & say the spell aloud while holding the crystal. Once complete, keep the crystal in your pocket or bag.

16) Write Your Own Spells

A Spell for: _____

Moon; _____

Ingredients/Materials required; _____
_____
_____

Spell;
_____
_____
_____
_____

Instructions;
_____
_____
_____
_____

A Spell for: _____

Moon; _____

Ingredients/Materials required; _____
_____
_____

Spell;
_____
_____
_____

Instructions;
_____
_____
_____
_____

A Spell for: _____

Moon; _____

 Ingredients/Materials required; _____
_____
_____

 Spell;
_____
_____
_____
_____

Instructions;
_____
_____
_____
_____

A Spell for: _____

Moon; _____

 Ingredients/Materials required; _____
_____
_____

 Spell;
_____
_____
_____
_____

Instructions;
_____
_____
_____
_____

A Spell for: _____

Moon; _____

Ingredients/Materials required; _____
_____
_____

Spell;
_____
_____
_____
_____

Instructions;
_____
_____
_____
_____

A Spell for: _____

Moon; _____

Ingredients/Materials required; _____
_____
_____

Spell;
_____
_____
_____
_____

Instructions;
_____
_____
_____
_____

A Spell for: _____

Moon; _____

 Ingredients/Materials required; _____
_____
_____

 Spell;
_____
_____
_____
_____

Instructions;
_____
_____
_____
_____

A Spell for: _____

Moon; _____

 Ingredients/Materials required; _____
_____
_____

 Spell;
_____
_____
_____
_____

Instructions;
_____
_____
_____
_____

A Spell for: _____

Moon; _____

 Ingredients/Materials required; _____
_____
_____

 Spell;
_____
_____
_____
_____

 Instructions;
_____
_____
_____
_____

A Spell for: _____

Moon; _____

 Ingredients/Materials required; _____
_____
_____

 Spell;
_____
_____
_____

 Instructions;
_____
_____
_____
_____

A Spell for: _____

Moon; _____

Ingredients/Materials required; _____
_____
_____

Spell;
_____
_____
_____
_____

Instructions;
_____
_____
_____
_____

A Spell for: _____

Moon; _____

Ingredients/Materials required; _____
_____
_____

Spell;
_____
_____
_____
_____

Instructions;
_____
_____
_____
_____

Arty Activity

This is your space to create freely!

17) Hexes, Curses & Karma

Not all spells are positive. Sometimes we have to cast to make people leave us alone, return their negative energy to them, or to teach them a lesson. This next part will explain this aspect of Magick, and how to be responsible and cast with great care.

Let's start with the difference between a Hex & a Curse.
A **Hex** usually includes causing mild to moderate harm, generally making life difficult, temporarily, until the receiver backs off.
A **Curse** is something that once you have it, unless you can find a counter-spell, you have it forever. Curses are life changing, sometimes can be passed down through generations, and should only be used for extremely good reason AND as a very last resort.

Karma is the natural consequences of our behaviour. Some Witches choose not to punish bad people, because they believe that the universe will ensure they get the "Karma" they have created for themselves. Other Witches prefer to speed up the process.

Here are some basic Hexes & Banishments to give you a better understanding of what they involve and how they work. This Magick is not to be taken lightly or treated as a joke. **Cast responsibly.**

A Spell That Binds Ill Intent

Ingredients/Materials required; Paper, pen, heatproof bowl or container, matches, dried sage & fresh mint.

Spell; *"Your ill intent be bound to you. No harm to others can it do. Purge it now and set it right. Send this darkness to the light."*

Instructions; Write the attackers name on the paper, then scrunch it up with the herbs inside it. Set the paper alight and place it quickly & carefully in the bowl. While the herbs are burning, say the spell.

A Spell That Breaks a Bond

Ingredients/Materials required; Heatproof pad, a black candle, a white candle, matches, string.

Spell; *"I remove this tie and all it's strife. It's time to move on with my life. The Maiden, Mother, Crone & me. As I will it, so mote it be."*

Instructions; Carve your name into the white candle, & the name of the person you no longer wish to be tied to in the black one. Stand them a couple of inches apart, & tie either end of the string to each candle. As you light the wicks, say the spell aloud twice. When the fire reaches the string, it will burn, & when it breaks, the spell is complete. Bury the ashes. Run used matches under water before binning.

A Freezer Spell (To Silence a Gossiper)

Ingredients/Materials required; Bay leaf, marker pen, freezable container, Storm Water.

Spell; *"Silence your words & hold your tongue, make amends to those you've stung, feel the weight of your own ill-will, your viciousness will quickly chill."*

Instructions; Write the attackers name on the bay leaf, put it in the freezer bag with a splash of Storm Water, say the spell while holding the bag, & put the bag in your freezer. Then enjoy the silence!

18) Write Your Own Hexes!

A Hex for: _____

Ingredients/Materials required; _____
_____
_____

Spell;
_____
_____
_____
_____

Instructions;
_____
_____
_____
_____

A Hex for: _____

Ingredients/Materials required; _____
_____
_____

Spell;
_____
_____
_____
_____

Instructions;
_____
_____
_____
_____

A Hex for: _____

Ingredients/Materials required; _____
_____
_____

Spell;
_____
_____
_____

Instructions;
_____
_____
_____
_____

A Hex for: _____

Ingredients/Materials required; _____
_____
_____

Spell;
_____
_____
_____

Instructions;
_____
_____
_____
_____

A Hex for: _____

Ingredients/Materials required; _____
_____
_____

Spell;
_____
_____
_____
_____

Instructions;
_____
_____
_____
_____

A Hex for: _____

Ingredients/Materials required; _____
_____
_____

Spell;
_____
_____
_____
_____

Instructions;
_____
_____
_____
_____

19) Sigil Magick; A Basic Understanding

Sigils are intentions in symbolic form. They are created by turning wishes into words, words into writing, & writing into pictures. Sounds simple enough, right? Let's break it down a step at a time & see exactly how it works, then you can give it a try yourself.

Step 1; Wishes into words

First you must think about your intention, your request. It could be something like *"I really wish I had more pocket money"*, *"I want to pass that test at school"*, or *"I would like to have more friends"*.

Step 2; Words into writing

Write your intention out in the PRESENT tense in as few words as possible. Let's use the school test as our example. At this stage, instead of writing "I want to pass", you'd write: "I PASS".

Step 3: Writing into pictures

First, cross out any vowels – A, E, I, O & U. They're not needed.

I PASS

Next, cross out any letters that repeat themselves.

P SS

Then you need to break the remaining letters down into their shapes.

PS = I) C)

Step 4: Turning the shapes into a Sigil

Create an image from the shapes left. Similar shapes should overlap each other to increase their power. See how the Sigil here looks a bit like a trophy? A trophy you might get for passing an important test? What a coincidence.

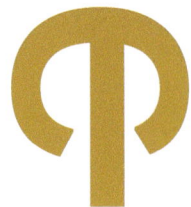

20) Create Your Own Sigil!

Step 1; Wishes into words

Step 2; Words into writing

Step 3: Writing into pictures

First, cross out any vowels – A, E, I, O & U. They're not needed.

Next, cross out any letters that repeat themselves.

Then you need to break the remaining letters down into their shapes.

Step 4: Turning the shapes into a Sigil

Create an image from the shapes left. Similar shapes should overlap each other to increase their power.

20) Create Your Own Sigil!

Step 1; Wishes into words

Step 2; Words into writing

Step 3: Writing into pictures

First, cross out any vowels – A, E, I, O & U. They're not needed.

Next, cross out any letters that repeat themselves.

Then you need to break the remaining letters down into their shapes.

Step 4: Turning the shapes into a Sigil

Create an image from the shapes left. Similar shapes should overlap each other to increase their power.

20) Create Your Own Sigil!

Step 1; Wishes into words

Step 2; Words into writing

Step 3: Writing into pictures

First, cross out any vowels - A, E, I, O & U. They're not needed.

Next, cross out any letters that repeat themselves.

Then you need to break the remaining letters down into their shapes.

Step 4: Turning the shapes into a Sigil

Create an image from the shapes left. Similar shapes should overlap each other to increase their power.

21) Divination (mancy galore!)

There are a huge number of forms of divination, more than you can shake a wand at! Unfortunately we don't have the time or space to name every single form of divination in this Grimoire, so we're just going to discuss the **5 most common forms.**

Cartomancy. A pack of (usually 78) Tarot cards with very unique designs on each one. Each image tells the readers' past, present & potential future. The deck is shuffled & then laid out a few of the cards in a special pattern called a "spread." The meaning of any card is modified according to it's place in the spread, the cards around it, & whether it was upside down!

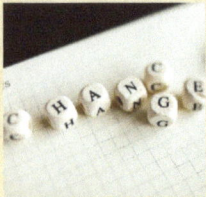

Cleromancy. Dice with letters instead of numbers are cast onto the table or a decorative board, & messages are read from any words spelled out. These dice contain all letters of the alphabet including multiple vowels, & sometimes numbers too. Also known as Cubomancy.

Chiromancy. The study of the shape of the hands, lines on the palms, and the mounds & creases of the fingers in order to read a person's personality, health & future, including how long they might live! The lines read include the Heart Line, Head Line, Fate Line, & Life Line.

Pendulum Scrying. A crystal hanging on a chain or string over a word board, which swings & sways in order to convey messages. The board can be simple with just "Yes" & "No" on it, or it can be complex with the alphabet & numbers as well as a few basic words on it.

Tasseomancy. Also known as interpreting patterns in tea leaves or coffee grounds left behind in the bottom of the mug after the drink has been drunk, & turning those patterns into messages from the spirits. This form of divination is also known as Tasseography or Tassology, & is a popular tradition practiced by the Romani Culture.

22) Auras: How To Read Them (And What They Mean)

An aura is the energy field that surrounds a person, an animal or a plant. It acts as a luminous shell that surrounds a physical body. Each person has their own aura which gives off it's own colour.

To see your own aura, start with rubbing your hands together faster & faster until they become warm with energy.

Then face a white wall (or a mirror) and lift your hand up in front of you with your thumb & index finger as close together as possible without touching, then let your eyes relax & your vision go out of focus.

Begin moving your thumb & index finger apart from each other slowly, then bringing it back, then apart again, like you've got a sticky substance between them that you're trying to get a better look at. After a few seconds, you'll see a colour appear between your finger/thumb & all around your hand, like a border - that's your aura!

Each person's aura has it's own colour. Once you've worked out your unique colour, use the following chart to figure out it's meaning.

The 6 most common aura colours, which are very similar to the chakras, are; Red, Orange, Yellow, Green, Blue & Purple.

Red symbolizes passion, strong-will, leadership & determination. Those with red auras tend to think very analytically, which allows them to overcome tough challenges. They also get easily frustrated, have fiery tempers, & can be selfish. They seize opportunities!

Orange symbolizes emotion, creativity, & healing. Those with orange auras love to help others, forming big communities. They also get easily anxious, get overwhelmed by negative thoughts & have a lot of mental & physical health issues. They're very intuitive.

Yellow symbolizes joy, imagination, knowledge & inspiration. They love to learn, to teach, to guide, & to help others in their intellectual journeys. They can however get easily depressed, & ignore their calling, instead isolating themselves. They're inspirational.

Green symbolizes harmony, empathy, peace & balance. They seek harmony between the spiritual realm & the physical world, healing as they go. They don't take to change very well though, ignoring their own inner turmoil. They respect Nature above all else.

Blue means communication, inspiration, healing & truth. This colour represents going with the flow while making their voices heard via writing, singing, or art. They are loyal, sometimes to their own detriment, & are very easily hurt emotionally. They're honest too.

Purple is for dedication, power & spirituality. Natural born leaders with great influence & a desire to help guide others to spiritual greatness. They can also be controlling & manipulative sometimes, but very wise.

There are 6 rarer aura colours, which are not seen as often. They are; Pink, Silver, Gold, Brown, Turquoise & White.

Pink is a gentle, loving, supportive, motherly type. They are supportive, very patient. They're comforting & warm, making others feel safe. But they can be possessive, overprotective & clingy to the point where others feel a bit suffocated. They're highly organized.

Silver brings psychic ability, intuition, mediumship gift & sensitivity. This aura-bearer is down to earth & easy to talk to. They are humble & love to lift others up as often as possible. However, if they don't use their gifts, they will lose them. They're good listeners.

Gold represents intelligence with a heart of gold. They make money quite easily when they put their mind to it, but have expensive taste. Golds hold an unbelievable wealth of experience, but tend to be over-achievers, which takes it's toll on their health.

Brown signifies Grounding, a love of animals, an "old soul", & a harmony with Nature. They prefer to walk in the forest than socialize with humans, & are active. They tend to lead solitary lives & indulge in comfort foods, leading to dietary issues. They're very smart.

Turquoise signifies connection, inspiration, fulfillment & peace. They go with the flow & settle peacefully, & they frequently encounter "coincidences" which are actually their Spirit Guides keeping them on the Path. They do feel lost a lot, & become easily fearful.

White represents love, purity, focus & innocence. The folk with white auras are fairly new to the Path & just starting out on their Pagan journey. Like a blank canvas ready to be filled with brilliance & uniqueness, these souls can be fairly detached from the world.

Press Flowers Here

23) Totem Guides - Who's Your Spirit Animal?

Every individual has an Animal Spirit Guide. This Guide provides protection & direction on your Pagan Path, & is a reflection of the personality & characteristics of the charge it watches over. It offers insight into the subconscious, & brings very important messages that we need to hear to make the right choices. It helps us through life's struggles, & steers us to acknowledge our inner voice, our gut instinct, & our higher selves. They are our Guardians.

So how do you figure out who yours is?

Let's start with what you probably already know without even realizing it. Have you ever felt like you see the same animal over & over again? Perhaps on the way to school, or outside your kitchen window, or when you're out & about? Perhaps on tv, in magazines, YouTube adverts, in books or on social media? Perhaps, when you ask yourself the question; "What is my Spirit Animal?" a specific creature will instantly pop into your head? That, my dear little Witchling, could very well be your Animal Spirit Guide. Even if it's not what you expected, it's definitely there for a reason.

So let's go on a Guided Meditation together and see if your Animal Guide is ready to reveal itself to you. But first things first, you will need to **cast a Circle of protection around yourself**, as a portion of your conscious state will be leaving your physical body for this exercise, & we need to ensure you are physically & psychologically protected from any negative energies or otherworldly spirits with ill-intent. **Read Chapter 8 for more information on how to do this.**

Sit in the centre of your Circle of Protection. Make yourself comfy & focus on your breathing. In for 5 seconds. Out for 5 seconds. In your minds eye, see yourself surrounded by a gorgeous bright light, with a golden thread coming from your centre. You feel it gently tug, pulling you forward, so you start walking. It leads you, effortlessly, on a path of more golden threads, thousands of them, weaved together in the web of Life. Everyone you've ever known is connected to it. Every creature, every plant, every soul, & you.

You walk towards a doorway, still guided by the thread of golden light. When you reach it, you step through it. A cool breeze blows across your face, and as you look around, you realise you're in a forest. There are luscious ferns at your feet, & tall trees in every direction you gaze. It is a place of complete peace, calm, respect. You hear nothing but the leaves rustling in the wind. The golden thread tugs again gently, so you keep walking, stepping over the mushrooms & the brushes of green, which shimmer silver waves.

You reach a clearing which has a fallen log lay in the middle. It beckons you to come take a seat, so you do. You feel your feet connecting with the Earth below, and Will your Spirit Animal to reveal itself. You hear rustling in the bushes from your left, & out steps your creature guardian.

You see each other. You see that the other end of the golden thread that comes from your centre, ends in your Spirit Animals' centre. You are connected. You always have been. You always will be. You have found each other. You are a part of each other.

It turns away, & heads back into the overgrowth. You stand & begin walking back the way you came, across the sea of golden thread weaved together perfectly, & settle back into your body, still sitting in your Circle of Protection. Slowly, gently, begin wiggling your toes, your fingers, have a stretch, have a yawn, & bring yourself back to reality. Open your eyes. **Remember to close your Circle.**

Draw your Spirit Animal

What was it? Why do you think this is your Guardian? What do you know about this creature already? Do some research & figure out as much as you can about it. Add whatever you find out here!

24) Witchionary: The A-Z of Magickal Terms

Affirmation

The insistence that something is true, it exists, and you believe in it.

Air

The element of the East; associated with intuition, learning, thought, and knowledge.

Alchemy

Using herbs & spices to combine chemistry with magic & medicine.

Altar

A dedicated area where witches practice their craft & rituals.

Amulet

An object or good luck charm with magical powers of protection.

Anoint

To smear or rub something with magical oil or water.

Arcane

Ancient or secret wisdom of Witches & magical souls.

Astral Projection

When the soul leaves the body and enters the astral plane.

Astrology

The effects of the movements & placements of planets & stars.

Athame

A (blunt) ceremonial knife/blade used to channel & direct energy.

Aura

The life energy that surrounds the bodies of all living things. See chapter 22 for more information.

Banish

To magically send away or repel negative energies or entities.

Beltane

The 4th Sabbat, a celebration of love, friendship, & the thinning of the veil between us & the Fae. See chapter 3 for more information.

Besom

A decorative broomstick constructed of twigs tied to a sturdy stick.

Bind

To magically restrain a person's energy or intentions.

Book of Shadows

A book of instructions for magickal rituals and spells.

Brigid (Lady Brig)

The Goddess of poetry, healing, metal crafting, fertility & fire.

Cauldron

A pot made of metal, used for cooking & spell work.

Chalice

A vessel intended for ceremonial drinks. Represents Water Element.

Chakras

The energy centers in the body (see chapter 6).

Charm

An object that is thought to carry magic e.g. luck or protection.

Coven

A group of at least 3 witches who gather to practice witchcraft.

Craft

Short for 'Witchcraft' – how most witches refer to their practice.

Crone

The third & final aspect of the Triple Goddess, represented by an old woman; associated with wisdom & the waning moon.

Crystal

Solidified minerals from deep within the earth that hold magic.

Curse

Spoken words with the intention to cause harm. Use wisely.

Deity

A God or a Goddess, also known as a higher power in Pagan Culture.

Divination

Seeking knowledge of the future using your own intuition & insight.

Earth

The element of the North; associated with stability, wisdom, knowledge, strength, growth, prosperity.

Elements
Earth, Air, Fire, Water. Each corresponds to a direction.

Fae
A small fairy with magical powers; may be invisible or visible.

Familiar
A witch's helpful, guardian spirit; usually a pet or a spirit animal.

Fire
The element of the South; associated with creativity, destruction, passion and power.

Gaia
One of the most important deities in Pagan Culture, Mother Earth herself.

Grimoire
A book of spells, rituals, incantations & magickal instructions.

Handfasting
A symbolic, beautiful marriage ceremony for pagans & witches.

Hex
A spell or charm which is intended to bring mild/moderate harm.

Horned One
The masculine representative of the God & Goddess.

Imbolc
The 2nd Sabbat, symbolized by the first snowdrops of the year & the growth of new life. See chapter 3 for more information.

Incantation
A spoken spell intended to have an effect on a person or object.

Incense
A sweet-smelling spice stick that is burned for ritual work.

Invoke
To call on a spirit, deity or higher power for help/assistance.

Litha
The 5th Sabbat. Summer Solstice/Midsummer. Known as the longest day & shortest night of the year. See chapter 3 for more info.

Loki
The Norse God of mischief & trickery.

Lughnasadh
Also known as Lammas. The 6th Sabbat, called The First Harvest.
See chapter 3 for more information.

Lunar Magic
"Lunar" is another word for Moon. See chapter 4 for more info.

Mabon
The 7th Sabbat, called the Autumn Equinox. Falls in September, and
is known as the Last Harvest. See chapter 3 for more info.

Maiden
The first aspect of the Triple Goddess, represented by a young
woman; associated with learning & the waxing moon.

Mother
The second aspect of the Triple Goddess, represented by a
pregnant woman, associated with knowledge & the full moon.

Odin
the ultimate Norse god; the divinity of wisdom, culture, war, and the
dead.

Ostara
The 3rd Sabbat & spring equinox, this is the true origin of Easter.
See chapter 3 for more information.

Pagan
A person who worships nature instead of mainstream religions.

Pentacle
A five-point star (the elements) inside a circle (of protection).

Pentagram
A five-pointed star without the circle. A symbol of the elements.

Poppet
A doll that represents someone so you can cast spells on them.

Ritual
A performance of magic intended to bring about an intention.

Sabbats
The 8 celebrations that make up the Wheel of the Year.

Samhain
Also known as Halloween. The 8th Sabbat & thinning of the veil.

Scrying

Gazing into a crystal ball, a mirror, water, or flickering flames in order to tell the future, amongst many other forms. Sometimes involves tools like a crystal pendulum or tarot cards.

Sigil

A sigil is a symbol used to represent a desire or intention (see chapter 19 for more information).

Smudging

Burning sacred herbs to produce a cloud of smoke which is used to cleanse a space.

Triple Moon

Also known as the Triple Goddess. Represents the Maiden, Mother, & the Crone, it honours each stage of the life cycle.

Wand

A wooden rod used to channel energy, cast circles, & focus magic.

Water

The element of the West; associated with purification, intuition, compassion, creation & emotion.

Witches' Bells

A cluster of decorative chimes used to chase negative energy out of your space. Hang them on your door to keep out bad vibes.

Yule

The Winter Solstice, the shortest day, & the 1st Sabbat in the Wheel of the Year. See chapter 3 for more information.

Final Thoughts

The Old Ways are returning, and more & more folk are waking up to the power inside them. You are already ahead of the game, dear reader. Don't ever let modern society dull your shine - you are a force to be reckoned with, and with time & practice, you will perfect your Craft to a level of absolute awesomeness.

Blessed Be, Little Witchling 🖤